D0325221

PEE WEES
ON FIRST

OTHER BOOKS YOU WILL ENJOY:

PEE WEES ON FIRST

Judy Delton

Illustrated by Alan Tiegreen

A YEARLING BOOK

Published by
Bantam Doubleday Dell Books for Young Readers
a division of
Bantam Doubleday Dell Publishing Group, Inc.
1540 Broadway
New York, New York 10036

The trademarks Yearling® and Dell® are registered in the U.S. Patent and Trademark Office and in other countries.

ISBN: 0-440-40977-2

Printed in the United States of America

April 1995

10 9 8 7 6 5 4 3

CWO

For Ingrid van der Leeden,
who works so hard with me
on the Pee Wees

Contents

CHAPTER 1

Spring Things

"It's not *your* fault you're not handicapped," said Jody George kindly. He looked up at Molly Duff from his wheelchair.

How did Jody know what she was thinking? thought Molly. Was he like the fortune-teller she had seen on TV? He seemed to know that she envied his shiny wheelchair with a motor and brakes.

Molly didn't actually want to be handicapped, but she did like to ride in Jody's wheelchair. And he got so much attention! Everyone at the Pee Wee Scout meetings on Tuesdays made a big fuss over him, running and getting him cupcakes and soda pop and pencils. He could do all that himself, but everyone liked to help him. And Jody had great parties at his house. He had his own CD player, and he took lots of trips with his family.

"Let me take a turn pushing him now," demanded Roger White. He shoved Molly out of the way and grabbed the wheelchair. Mrs. Peters, their Scout leader, frowned at him. "Sit down, Roger," she said.

Maybe it wasn't the wheelchair Molly wanted. Maybe it was Jody himself Molly envied. He was kind and generous and funny. And he was rich and got to do things the other Pee Wees didn't do.

Whatever it was, Molly felt guilty. She had a nice home and good parents who loved her. She had her own little room with a new white canopied bed and a

white rocking chair with a ruffle on the seat. It was no wheelchair, but it was more suitable for her bedroom, her mother said.

Mrs. Peters rapped a spoon on the table. "Attention!" she called. "Today we have some news."

All of the Pee Wees stopped talking.

Roger stopped throwing plastic forks at Tim Noon.

They all sat down in their chairs and looked at Mrs. Peters.

When Mrs. Peters said "news" it could mean a party. Or a field trip. Or best of all, a new badge. Once, while they tried to earn a badge, they got caught in a blizzard and were rescued just in time, before they had to eat each other.

And once Mrs. Peters had told them she was going to have a baby! That was baby Nick, who sat in his high chair at the table with them right now.

But Mrs. Peters didn't look like she was going to have a baby.

And it was spring, there couldn't be any blizzard.

"This is sort of two-part news," she went on.

The Pee Wees cheered. Two-part news was even better than one-part news. Unless, of course, it was one of those "good news, bad news" things.

Rachel Meyers waved her hand. "Mrs. Peters," she called. "Is it a contest? My cousin's troop in Wisconsin entered a contest and won a refrigerator."

When everyone looked at her, puzzled, she added, "It makes these cute little ice cubes and everything."

"Who wants a refrigerator?" scoffed Roger. "We've got a refrigerator." He pointed upstairs to Mrs. Peter's kitchen.

"No, Rachel," said Mrs. Peters patiently. "The news isn't a contest."

"I'll bet it's the Fourth of July parade," said Patty Baker. She had a twin brother who was a Pee Wee too. His name was Kenny.

"We had that last year," said Sonny Stone. "I remember those horses."

Sonny's name used to be Betz until his mother married the fire chief, Larry Stone. Now Sonny had a real dad, and two babies, twins, a boy and a girl, who came on a plane from far away. Molly thought a father would help Sonny grow up, but it hadn't. He was still a mama's boy. He was the only one with training wheels still on his bike. Seven was too old for training wheels, Molly thought. The kids all laughed at him.

Mrs. Peters laughed. "No, it's not a parade," she said. "Today we'll talk about the first part of the surprise, and that's about the next badge we are going to earn."

6

"Yea!" shouted the Pee Wees. Roger stomped on the floor and whistled between his teeth.

They couldn't have too many badges, thought Molly. She already had lots of them. Badges for skiing and skating and baby-tending and horseback riding. Badges for acting and walking pets and camping. Even a badge for catching a fish and spotting a groundhog.

"Pretty soon our badges will cover our whole shirt!" said Mary Beth Kelly. She was Molly's best friend.

"They'll go up our sleeves!" said Tracy Barnes.

"And down our legs!" shouted Lisa Ronning.

"They'll be on top of our head," said Tim Noon.

"How could they be on our head, Noon?" said Kevin Moe. "That's dumb."

"Is not," said Tim.

"Is too," said Kevin Moe.

Mrs. Peters held up her hand.

"Mrs. Peters, what *do* we do when we run out of room to sew our badges?" asked Ashley Baker, frowning. Ashley was Patty and Kenny's cousin from California. She belonged to the Saddle Scouts there. But when she visited her cousins, she was a temporary Pee Wee Scout.

"We'll worry about that when we come to it," said their leader. "Right now we just want to think about how we'll earn this new badge. The badge is for something that happens in the spring. Can you guess what that is?"

The Pee Wees guessed.

"School is out in spring," said Lisa.

"We don't get a badge for that," Tracy said, laughing.

"We should," grumbled Roger. "It's the best thing that happens all year."

8

"In spring leaves come out on the trees," said Tim.

"We don't get a badge for that either," scoffed Mary Beth.

"A tree should get a badge for that!" Kevin laughed.

Molly thought about spring things. Gardens. Raking. Picnics. Ants.

"Is it an insect badge?" she asked. "Lots of bugs come out in spring."

"Yuck," said Rachel. "I definitely don't want a bug badge."

The boys started making creepy-crawler motions across the floor and the table. They tried to make bug noises.

"Spring does mean bugs," laughed Mrs. Peters. "But it is not a bug badge we're after. I'll give you a clue. It's a game. Where people eat hot dogs. And it starts with a *B*."

"Bingo!" shouted Sonny.

Everyone laughed and Sonny looked

9

hurt. "Bingo is a game that starts with a *B* and you eat hot dogs when you play. I'd like to get a Bingo badge."

"This game is played outdoors," said Mrs. Peters. "In a park. And sometimes you watch it on TV."

"It's baseball," said Jody. "I'll bet anything it is."

"Jody is right," said Mrs. Peters. "The Pee Wees are going to play ball! It's going to be 'batter up!' for Troop 23!"

CHAPTER 2

The VIP

"I hate sports," said Rachel. "My dad says there is too much interest in sports in this country."

"I don't know how to play baseball," whined Sonny.

"Everybody knows how to play baseball, dummy," said Roger. "It's one of those things you know when you're born."

"Sports are dangerous," said Ashley. "Once our neighbor got hit on the head with a baseball. He had to have stitches and everything."

A few more of the Pee Wees were complaining, but most of them were cheering.

"You won't get hurt at our ball game," said Mrs. Peters. "We will use a softer ball. Pee Wee baseball will be easier than real baseball. And it will be good exercise. It is something we can do outside and we can stretch our muscles and learn a skill at the same time. To earn the badge, you just have to have fun. You'll play in the game, and you'll hit the ball."

Mrs. Peters made it sound simple, thought Molly. Play a game, have fun, hit a ball. But if you couldn't hit a ball, it wouldn't be much fun!

"I play baseball all the time," said Roger. "I'm on a team with my cousins."

Now Molly began to worry. It sounded like most of the other Scouts knew more about baseball than she did. Roger sure did. And Kevin and Jody were smart at everything. But she was sure her best friend, Mary Beth, didn't know any more than she did.

"I've never played baseball," Molly confessed to her.

"My family plays on Saturdays when we have family picnics," Mary Beth said.

Rat's knees! Even her best friend could play! And even though Rachel and Ashley didn't like the game, she was sure they could play. They would probably hit a home run! She would be left with Sonny, holding the bat. And holding the wrong end!

"What do we do to get the badge?" asked Rachel. "What is the other part of the news? Part two?"

"The second part," said their leader, "is to keep a notebook or a scrapbook of baseball trivia. See how much you can find out about the history of the game, or about the players. You can save baseball cards in the book, and anything else you can find. You can go to the library and see if you can scout out facts that no one else knows."

Some of the Pee Wees were writing all this down in school notebooks, just the way they wrote their homework down. Molly liked lists and she liked notebooks. But she didn't have to write this down. She'd remember this. This was the easy part. Notebooks were fun, hitting a ball wasn't.

"I can hit a ball, but I don't like that stuff about notebooks," said Tim.

"Neither do I," said Roger. "I just want to hit a home run over the top of a tree." Roger swung an imaginary bat at an imaginary ball and spun around like the batters do on TV.

Mrs. Peters was talking about how baseball began. She told them about famous players and record-breaking home runs. She told them about outdoor games

and indoor domed stadiums. And then she told them how to play the game.

"The object is to hit the ball and run around the three bases to score a home run," she said.

She told them about pitching and scoring and strikeouts. And she held up pictures of a baseball field.

But Molly wasn't paying much attention. She was thinking about her note-scrapbook. She could put more than facts in it. She could draw pictures of baseball players. She could make her book the best one in the troop—the fattest and longest and neatest—and then Mrs. Peters would excuse her from hitting any balls.

"I wish we could either hit the ball or keep a notebook," said Tracy when Mrs. Peters was through talking. "Instead of doing both of them."

"I do too," said Roger.

Most of the Pee Wees wanted the "one thing" to be hitting a ball.

Others like Kevin couldn't wait to do them both.

But Molly was the only one who only wanted to do the scrapbook.

She wondered how Jody was going to hit a ball. How could he run around bases? Probably the pitcher would throw the ball really slow and right to him. They would make sure he hit it! Molly wished she were handicapped too. She *was* handicapped when it came to hitting a ball! If she were in a wheelchair, and everyone made a fuss over her, she bet she could hit the ball too. Jody was lucky. Someone would probably even push his chair around the bases. Rat's knees!

"I have some more news too," said Mrs. Peters. "This news is even more fun."

The Pee Wees cheered. Except Molly. She wasn't going to cheer ahead of time.

The news could be some other fun thing that really wasn't.

"There is a professional baseball player coming to town to scout out players for a new team," said Mrs. Peters. "He's retired now, and his name is Brett Brady. He's going to watch local games and round up talent."

"Hey, I've heard of him!" shouted Roger.

"Well," Mrs. Peters went on, "he has agreed to come and talk to us about the game while he's here! He'll tell us about his experiences playing ball. And he'll give us some tips."

"Yea!" shouted the Pee Wees.

"He's a VIP," confided Jody.

"What's a Vip?" whispered Mary Beth to Molly. "One of those things like Dracula that sucks blood?"

"That's a vampire," said Molly.

"A VIP means a very important person," said Ashley. "I know because my uncle is one."

Rat's knees, pooh to you, thought Molly.

"I'm sure Mr. Brady will be interesting to listen to," said Mrs. Peters. "He will help us get our badge, and give us lots of inside information about baseball! And now while we have our cupcakes, let's talk about good deeds."

Sonny's mother went upstairs to get the cupcakes and milk. She was the assistant troop leader.

Molly didn't want to think about good deeds. It was hard to think about good deeds when she was worried. And part one of this badge was a big worry.

CHAPTER 3

Dusting Baseballs

No one else seemed to have Molly's problem. They all forgot about baseball and waved their hands in the air to tell about how they flattened soda pop cans and recycled bottles and got cats out of trees and raked their yards. Jody had helped wash windows at his house, but Molly didn't know how exactly.

"I taught the twins how to read," said Sonny, with his mouth full of chocolate cupcake. He had a milk mustache.

"You did not," shouted Kenny. "Those babies are too little to read!"

21

"Are not," said Sonny.

"Are too," said Kenny. "They aren't even a year old!"

"Well, they look at my books when I hold them up," said Sonny.

"That's not reading, dummy," said Roger.

Mrs. Peters held up her hand for silence.

"It's not quite reading, perhaps," she said tactfully, "but it is a good deed to show your brother and sister a book."

"See?" growled Sonny.

"They just looked at the pictures, that's all they did," growled Roger back.

More hands waved. After Mrs. Peters had called on all of them, she said, "Molly, haven't you got a good deed to report?"

Molly was so surprised to hear her name, she said the first thing that came to her mind.

"I dusted the baseballs!" she cried.

Everyone burst into laughter. Even her best friend, Mary Beth!

"I mean baseboards," she said with a red face. "I dusted the baseboards in the livingroom for my mom. And the table legs."

Roger stood up and pretended to dust an imaginary baseball with his paper napkin. "Hey, you guys, look how shiny this baseball is!"

Now some of the other Pee Wees were dusting baseballs.

"What's a baseboard?" frowned Tim.

"Baseboards go around the walls," said Rachel. "Next to the floor."

Playing baseball must be a bigger worry than she had thought, for her to say something so dumb! It must have been the first thing on her mind. Molly wanted to get baseballs out of her mind.

Molly noticed that when everyone else

laughed at her, Kevin and Jody didn't. Molly liked them both. She had always planned to marry Kevin when she grew up. When the Pee Wees recycled, she had even made a wedding dress out of an old curtain.

But since Jody joined the Pee Wees, she wasn't sure about marrying Kevin. Jody was awfully nice too, and awfully smart. She made up her mind not to rush into anything.

The Scouts joined hands and sang their Pee Wee Scout song. Molly loved the song but she didn't hear many of the words this time. She mostly just heard Roger laughing. Laughing at dusting baseballs. Laughing when she tried to hit a ball in the park.

On the way home, good deeds were forgotten and everyone talked about the VIP.

"I'm going to make sure he sees me play," said Roger. "Maybe I'll get chosen for that big-league team he's scouting for."

Ashley stopped in the middle of the sidewalk.

"You?" she said, laughing. "It isn't a Pee Wee team he wants! He's looking for grown-up players!"

Roger turned red. "I knew that," he said. "But I'm big for my age."

That was true, thought Molly. Roger was the tallest Pee Wee Scout. But that didn't mean he was old enough to play grown-up baseball! He was still only seven!

"Anyway, when he sees how good I am, he'll start another team. A Pee Wee league. Or else he'll put my name on the list for when I'm grown up."

"I wish he'd discover me too," said Sonny.

Now not only Ashley laughed, everyone did.

"You still can't ride a two-wheel bike," said Lisa. "If you play baseball like you ride a bike, you haven't got a chance even in the baby league."

"Baseball with training wheels!" chanted Roger. Some of the others joined in.

Poor Sonny, thought Molly. But why did he say such dumb things? Still, Molly herself said dumb things sometimes. Like dusting baseballs. Sometimes you couldn't help it. Probably even Mrs. Peters and Brett Brady said dumb things sometimes. Maybe even her parents!

Mary Beth and Molly waved good-bye to the others, and turned at their corner.

"We can practice tomorrow after school," said Mary Beth. "I've got a bat and a softball."

"I can't hit a ball!" said Molly.

"How do you know?" asked Mary

Beth. "You just think you can't. You haven't tried lately, have you?"

Molly shook her head. "I did when I was five," she said.

"Well we're a lot older now. Just wait and see."

Molly said good-bye and went in the house and told her mom and dad the awful news.

"I like the notebook part," she said.

"You'll be able to play ball," said her dad. "It just takes a little practice. And remember, the old Ace here can help you. I wasn't the star pitcher in college for nothing."

"I don't remember that," said Mrs. Duff, smiling.

"Well, maybe not the *star*," said her dad.

By the time they ate dinner, Molly had forgotten baseball. Mary Beth would help her. She ate her lasagna and told her mom and dad about Sonny teaching the twins to read. They all laughed, until her dad got the newspaper and opened it up. On the front page it said, BRETT BRADY IN TOWN TO SCOUT FOR HITTERS.

Molly helped clear the table, and then she fed her dog, Skippy. She went to her room and did her homework. Then she took out a new notebook and wrote *What I Know About Baseball* on the cover. Then she got her pajamas on and brushed her teeth. She said good night to her parents and got into bed. As soon as she went to sleep, she dreamed that Brett Brady came to her door and asked her dad to play on the new big-league team. Her mother said he wasn't a star player, but that Molly was! Brett gave Molly a uniform and a bat and a ball and when they got to the ballpark, Roger was on first base! Mary Beth was the pitcher, and Kevin was running around all the bases pushing Jody in his wheelchair. In her dream, Molly tried to lift the bat to hit the ball, but it was too heavy. Instead of hitting the bat, the ball hit Molly on the head!

"Rat's knees!" she was saying as she woke up. "I *told* you I couldn't hit the ball!"

In the morning she got up and got dressed, and hoped her dream wasn't going to come true in the park after school.

CHAPTER 4

Baby Ruth

"Okay," said Mary Beth. "This is the way you hold the bat."

Mary Beth swung the bat loosely between her knees. The girls were in the park, where there was a lot of room to hit balls. There were some children in a sandbox, and some mothers pushing strollers. There was a dog chasing a Frisbee too. It felt good to be outside in spring. The sun made the top of her head warm.

"Now you throw me the ball," said Mary Beth. "Stand back there and be the pitcher."

Molly threw the ball. It didn't go any-where near Mary Beth. It went closer to the dog, who stopped chasing the Frisbee and went after the ball.

"He thinks you are playing fetch with him," laughed his master.

The dog brought the ball back to Molly and dropped it at her feet. The ball was wet.

"Throw it right here," called Mary Beth, pointing to the ground beside her. "This doesn't look like home plate, but it is. Just pretend."

This time the ball Molly threw fell to the ground and rolled to the middle of the park into a little puddle.

Mary Beth sighed. Molly could hear her. It seemed that Molly couldn't even throw a ball, let alone *hit* one!

Mary Beth ran and got the ball out of the water and threw it to Molly. She missed it. Things did not look good.

The next time Molly threw the ball, it went closer to Mary Beth. It went right to her swinging bat. And the bat hit the ball so hard, it flew out of the park and across the street into someone's backyard. Mary Beth ran around the three imaginary bases and said, "That was a home run for my team."

So pitching well was bad too! If Molly threw a good pitch, the other team could get a home run and win the game!

Mary Beth ran to get the ball.

"Now it's your turn," she said, handing Molly the bat. Molly swung it back and forth the way her friend had. It felt heavy. Like in her dream! And it was so thin! How could anyone hit a ball with such a thin stick?

Mary Beth threw the ball to her. Molly swung the bat at it but missed it.

"See?" she said. "I told you I can't hit the ball."

"You just need practice," said Mary Beth. "You are new at this."

Mary Beth pitched the ball again.

Molly missed the ball again.

Mary Beth tried once more.

And Molly missed it once more.

"It's too thin!" shouted Molly. "Why don't they make bats fatter?"

A few people gathered around the girls to watch. Some of them were Pee Wee Scouts. One was Roger!

"Go away!" she said to him.

"It's a public park," said Roger. "You can't make me go away."

He sat down on the grass as if he intended to stay for good.

"Batter up!" he shouted. "Let's see some action!"

The only action Roger would see, thought Molly, was the girls leaving.

She handed the bat to Mary Beth.

"I'm no good," she said.

"Don't give up so fast," said Mary Beth. "We can go over to my house and play."

Roger got up and began to follow the girls, but Mary Beth told him her yard was private property and she would call the police if he went in it.

"Ho, ho, I'm really scared," he scoffed. But Molly noticed he didn't follow them.

In Mary Beth's backyard Molly could not hit the ball either.

Or in the empty lot next door. Even when Mary Beth stood really close and almost set the ball on top of her bat.

"I'm going to get a fatter bat," said Molly.

"They don't make them fatter than this," said Mary Beth.

"Maybe I'll make my own," said Molly.

Molly said good-bye, and went home. She gave Skippy a run. She even threw him a ball. *He* caught it with no problem. Then she looked in her garage for something to make a fat bat out of. There were rakes and hoes and gardening shears. There was a lawn mower and a snow-plow. But there was nothing to make a bat from.

Rat's knees, she thought. It's not easy to find a fat bat. She would do it later. Right now she would get her notebook and go to the library. At least she could do that.

She looked in the encyclopedia under *baseball*.

A game has nine innings, the article said. Molly wrote that down. She wondered what an inning was. It must be the opposite of an outing. An outing was like a picnic or a hot dog roast.

She wrote down *home run* and *grand slam* and *rain check*.

She wrote down *bunt* and *bench* and *bases*.

Home plate is made of white rubber, she read. She had never heard of a rubber plate, but the book must be telling the truth. Authors didn't lie.

Farther on it said that the baseball was made of leather, with twine-covered cork inside! What a funny place for a ball of yarn! She had never seen a ball of yarn anywhere but in her grandma's knitting basket.

Another book had lots of "amazing baseball facts."

Someone named Baby Ruth had hit 714 home runs. Molly didn't remember seeing any women on the baseball teams her dad watched on TV. But Ruth must have been on a team if she hit all those home runs. And she must be very young to be called "baby." If she could do it, maybe there was a chance for Molly herself, and for Sonny. He was a baby if anyone was! She would have to remember to tell Sonny at the next meeting. She wrote it all down in her notebook. Then she drew pictures of balls and home plates and even some baseball players. She drew a picture of Baby Ruth. She even made up a story about a girl in a wheelchair who could not hit the ball with a thin bat. She would have the best baseball book of all! Even if she couldn't hit the ball.

CHAPTER 5

Acting Casual

The next afternoon the Pee Wees practiced in the park. Afterward, Roger said, "I'm going to find that guy Brett Brady. I'm going to show him how good I can play."

"He'll make a fool of himself," whispered Mary Beth.

"I wonder what this Brady guy looks like," said Kenny.

"He's real tall and he's got glasses," said Sonny. "I saw him on TV a long time ago."

"He's got black hair," said Tim. "And it's real curly."

"How do you know?" demanded Jody.

Tim shrugged. "Someone told me," he said.

"I wonder where he's staying when he's here," said Kevin. "We could go find him and hit a few balls while he's watching."

"Maybe he is staying with somebody he knows," said Lisa.

"I don't think he knows anybody here," said Ashley. "His friends probably live in big cities where there are big ball teams. You know, major leagues."

"When you're from out of town, you stay at a hotel," said Rachel.

"There's a hotel downtown," said Patty. "A big one."

"Hey, I'm going to go find him," said Roger.

The Pee Wees followed Roger. They all

wanted to see Brett Brady. They all wanted to see a famous person.

Molly wanted to get a head start finding out more baseball facts. Facts that came from a real player, instead of from a book or even from Mrs. Peters. Maybe he knew this Baby Ruth! Maybe he knew why she was named after a candy bar!

Some of the others wanted Brett Brady to see how well they played.

Roger wanted to get signed up for a team!

When the Pee Wees got to the hotel, they were all out of breath from running. They sat on a bench in front of the building to rest.

"We can't miss him here," said Mary Beth. "If he goes in or out, we'll see him."

The Pee Wees sat on the bench a long time. They watched and watched for Brett Brady to walk by.

"What are you going to say when you see him?" Jody asked Roger.

"I'll just grab him and say, 'Hey, come and watch me hit some grand slams,'" said Roger.

"I don't think we should let him know we know who he is," said Kevin. "That might scare him off. Everybody wants to get chosen. You have to be cool and let him discover us."

"That's smart," said Ashley. "To act casual about it."

"Well, maybe," said Roger. "Just keep our balls and bats out in plain view. When he sees them he'll know we are pros. No one else would walk around with bats and balls."

"Hey, here comes a guy!" whispered Lisa.

A man came out the door.

He was tall.

He had glasses.

But he didn't have dark curly hair.

He was bald.

"Brett isn't bald," whispered Tracy. "It's not him."

The next person who came out was a woman.

Then two men went in. One was short and fat. The other one was limping.

"Does Brett limp?" asked Tim.

"Naw," said Roger. "He couldn't run around those bases very fast if he limped."

"Handicapped people play ball," Jody reminded them.

"He could have hurt his leg in a ball game," said Mary Beth.

"Maybe that's why he retired," said Kenny.

By that time the men were out of sight.

"I have to go," said Jody. "My dad is picking me up at the library."

Some of the other Pee Wees had to leave too. Soon only Molly and Mary Beth and Roger and Sonny were left.

"I'm not moving till I see this guy," said Roger.

Molly felt the same way. This was her chance to get the inside scoop on Baby Ruth.

"It's good those guys are gone," said Sonny. "Now we get a better chance to get chosen for his team."

More time went by, and Molly almost fell asleep in the warm sun. Suddenly, Mary Beth nudged her in the ribs.

"Look!" she said. "That's him!"

A tall man was coming down the street. He had dark curly hair. He wore glasses. He did not limp. And he was carrying a big package.

"Baseballs!" said Roger. "He's got baseballs in there!"

"Or else trophies he's won," said Sonny.

"What do we do?" said Mary Beth.

"Act casual, like Ashley said," said Molly.

The Pee Wees yawned. Roger got up and swung a bat.

Sonny tossed a ball in the air and caught it.

As the man got closer, the Pee Wees casually blocked his path. The man couldn't get by.

"Hi, kids!" he said. "You baseball players?"

Now Molly knew he was their man!

"You bet!" said Roger. "Batter up!"

The man tried to walk around Roger, and bumped into Sonny.

"I think I'd like a candy bar," said Molly clearly. "Maybe a *Baby Ruth*."

She looked at the man's face. He smiled! He knew! But she must remember to be casual.

Sonny tossed a ball to the man. He caught it and tossed it back.

"The park might be a better place to play ball," said the man. "It's hard to play in the middle of the sidewalk."

"He's right!" shouted Sonny. "Let's go!"

Roger grabbed one of the man's arms, and Sonny grabbed the other. The man tried to pull away, but the boys held on. Roger was strong. And Sonny was wiry. No one wanted Brett to get away.

CHAPTER 6

A Pee Wee Error

Brett didn't seem to want to go to the park, thought Molly. He kept trying to escape. Molly and Mary Beth ran along in front of him, turning around to talk.

"You don't happen to know Baby Ruth, do you?" asked Molly politely. And casually.

"Baby Ruth?" he asked. He looked puzzled.

"He has to pretend he doesn't know anything about baseball," Molly whis-

pered to Mary Beth. "So we won't know who he is. He's playing dumb."

Mary Beth nodded. "He's doing a good job of it," she whispered back.

"Baby Ruth, Baby Ruth," sang Molly. "Have you ever heard of Baby Ruth?"

"The ballplayer?" asked Brett. "Babe Ruth?"

Now they were making progress! It *was* Brett! No one else would know about Baby Ruth, the little girl ballplayer who was named after a candy bar!

"Babe or Baby," said Molly. "Did you ever play with her?"

Now the man looked worried. Molly's question seemed to bother him! He pulled away from Sonny and Roger. As he did, his package of baseballs and trophies fell to the ground. The package opened, but what fell out were not baseballs or trophies.

What fell out were lots and lots of papers. Papers with writing on them, and people's names. Papers that said ACME IN-SURANCE AGENCY at the top.

A sandwich fell out too. It was wrapped in waxed paper and it smelled like tuna fish.

Brett scrambled to pick everything up. The Pee Wees helped.

"I'm an insurance salesman," said the man.

"He's just saying that," whispered Mary Beth to Molly. "To put us off. He doesn't want to let us know who he really is. That's why he carries around these fake papers."

"Sure, sure, you're an insurance salesman!" said Roger, winking at the man in a knowing way. Sonny winked too.

Roger sidled up to the man. When he got close, he whispered, "We all know you really aren't an insurance man, don't we?"

Molly took Roger aside.

"We could pretend to buy some insurance," she said. "We could play along with him, and then we could work in some baseball questions."

"I don't think we have to do that," said Roger. "I think he can tell us who he really is. Hey, we won't blow your cover," he said, jabbing the man in the ribs in a confidential way.

Now the man looked nervous. It was true the Pee Wees were on to him, but it wasn't as if he were a crook or something, thought Molly. There was nothing to be embarrassed about just because you were a retired baseball player.

"Being a ballplayer is nothing to be ashamed of," said Molly kindly.

"Lots of people play ball," said Sonny.

"You're going to speak at our Scout meeting on Tuesday," Roger confessed.

"We just wanted you to see us play first."

"And we wanted you to answer some questions," said Molly.

Brett looked confused. Just then a man came up to him and said, "There you are, Roland! I've been waiting at the office for you. Our meeting starts in five minutes! This is our chance to insure all of those airport workers!"

Roland? Airport workers? What was happening here?

The Pee Wees were stunned. "He really *is* an insurance man!" said Molly.

"That's what I told you," grumbled Roland.

"Why didn't you tell us you weren't Brett?" demanded Mary Beth, stamping her foot.

"You lied to us!" said Sonny.

"He didn't lie," said Molly. "He never said he was Brett."

Roland brushed his suit off and straightened his papers.

"I'm sorry I'm late," he said to the man. "These kids are crazy! They kept calling me Brett!"

How could the Pee Wees have made such a mistake? What made them think Roland was Brett? Poor Roland, thought Molly. It wasn't his fault they thought he was Brett. And now they had made him late for a meeting!

"We have to apologize," whispered Molly to Mary Beth. She knew Roger would never say he was sorry. It was up to the girls.

"It was our fault," said Mary Beth. "We thought you were someone else."

"We're sorry we made you late," added Molly.

Roland patted Molly on the head and muttered that it was all right. He looked like he just wanted to get away from the

Pee Wees as fast as he could. He walked off down the street to his insurance meeting. The Pee Wees started for home, feeling rather low.

"What a waste of time," said Sonny. "I still think he tricked us."

When Molly got home, the phone was ringing. Sonny had told his mother about Roland, and she had called Mrs. Peters. Mrs. Peters told the Duffs the story.

"You know," said Molly's dad, "you children should not have talked to strangers."

"That's right," said Molly's mother. "Roland could have been a criminal and had a weapon," she went on, "and kidnapped you or Sonny."

"Who'd want Sonny?" muttered Molly. "And we needed to meet Brett and talk to him."

Molly wasn't sure she knew the difference between being a good Scout getting information for her badge, and being a careless Scout, talking to strangers and being kidnapped.

The story got back to all the Scouts, and Rachel called Molly, and then Ashley called her. After that Jody called.

"I'm glad you're safe," he said. "You could have been kidnapped!"

Jody liked her! He was glad she was safe! But maybe he would have been glad for any of the Pee Wees. Maybe he had called Mary Beth, too! Jody was a nice person. He liked everyone, not just Molly. Still, it was nice of him to be glad she was safe.

CHAPTER 7

The Real Brett Brady (And the Real Baby Ruth)

At the next Pee Wee meeting, some of the Scouts brought their scrapbooks. Kevin's was big, but not as big as Molly's.

Molly's was the biggest. It had the most pictures and the most facts, and it was the only one with real stories in it. Mrs. Peters held it up for the class.

"This is a fine job!" said Mrs. Peters. "It looks like Molly has half her badge already."

Rat's knees. Half a badge. It sounded

like even a fat notebook would not be enough. She would have to hit a ball.

"Hey, I've got as much stuff as Molly does," said Roger. "I'll bet she doesn't know what home plate is made out of."

"I do too," said Molly. "Rubber."

"Well, I'll bet you don't know how much a baseball weighs," he said.

"Five ounces is regulation," said Molly.

All the Pee Wees clapped. Roger looked as red as Roland the insurance man had looked.

Then there was a knock at the door. Mrs. Stone went upstairs to answer it. When she came down, she said, "Boys and girls, this is Brett Brady!"

A man who was not tall and dark walked into the room.

His hair was not curly. And not black. It was gray and white.

"Hi," he said to Troop 23. "I'm Brett

Brady and I hear you thought I was an insurance salesman!"

Some of the Pee Wees looked embarrassed. Molly jumped to her feet.

"We didn't think *you* were Roland," she said. "We thought Roland was you. I mean . . ."

Brett laughed. "I was just joking," he said.

Molly sat down. She had not said that right. But Brett Brady didn't seem upset. He told them about his days on the team. He told about the home runs he had hit. He told them funny stories about the players and the fans. And he answered their questions.

"Hey, who was the fastest pitcher ever?" shouted Roger.

"That was Nolan Ryan," said Brett. "He pitched a ball recorded at one hundred miles an hour in 1974 for the California Angels."

"I knew that," said Molly. "It's in my scrapbook!"

Brett answered more questions. He told them that baseball's longest game was 33 innings, and had to be continued at a later date. He told them that one famous ballplayer for St. Louis named Pete Gray only had one arm.

Tim put one arm behind his back and pretended to swing a bat with the other. Soon all the Pee Wees were playing one-armed baseball. Mrs. Peters had to tell them to be quiet and sit down.

Molly wanted to ask Brett about Baby Ruth, but she didn't get a chance. The meeting was over, and everyone followed Brett outside to hit balls for him and try to get on his team. The boys were knocking each other over to be first in line. Brett showed them all how to hold a bat the professional way. And how to hit the ball. But he didn't sign Roger up

for his team, or any of the other Pee Wees.

After Brett had left, Mrs. Peters talked a little more about baseball, and said, "On Saturday we will have our big game in the park. The parents will play Troop 23. It will be a chance for you all to hit the ball and get your badge."

There it was again. Hitting the ball. It was getting close to badge time, and without a fat bat Molly was doomed.

When she got home, her dad seemed to read her mind. "Let's go out in the yard and hit some balls," he said after dinner. "Let me show you how the old Ace can hit a home run."

"Not through our kitchen window," warned Molly's mother.

Mr. Duff looked shocked. "Of course not!" he said.

In the yard, he set up three bases with some rocks. Skippy watched him.

"Now when I hit the ball, I run to first base, then second, then third, then home," he explained.

Molly threw him the ball. He didn't hit it.

She threw it again. This time he hit it and it went over their garage. Her dad dashed around all three bases. Skippy ran after him.

"Go, Skippy!" Molly cried. Maybe her dad would forget about teaching her baseball.

"Now usually there would be players on the bases or in the field to catch the ball and put me out," he said. "But if they didn't, I'd make a home run."

Now it was Molly's turn. "Keep your eye on the ball," he said.

Molly did. But it didn't help. She missed the ball. Then she missed it again.

Then her dad moved up closer so

she would be sure to hit it. But it flew by Molly and rolled across the lawn. Skippy caught it and brought it over to Molly.

"Good dog," she said. Skippy dropped the ball on her foot.

Her dad was a good pitcher, Molly thought, and a good teacher, so it must be Molly who was a bad student. All she could hope was that by Saturday it would rain. Hard. And they wouldn't be able to play.

"Chin up!" said her dad. "There are worse things in the world than not being a good ballplayer."

He might be right, but Molly wanted that badge. If only she could find a fatter bat!

And then she saw it! When she hung her sweater up in the closet, there was something lying on the shelf she had not noticed before! It was like a bat, but it was fatter than a bat! It looked like the answer to her problem! She took it down and put it into a bag.

On Saturday the sun was shining brightly. The Pee Wees gathered in the park. Molly had her bag with her.

Sonny was the only one with a baseball uniform on. It said DODGERS on the back of it. It was too big for Sonny.

"Hey, what are you going to dodge, Stone?" yelled Roger.

Mr. Peters put an old pie pan where home plate was. Then he put a sandbag on each base.

"Now nine of us will play nine of you," he said.

There were more than nine parents there. And more than nine Pee Wees. There were thirteen Pee Wees! Thirteen minus nine left four! Maybe Molly could be one of the four who did not have to get up to bat! But if she did, it wouldn't matter, she thought. With her fat bat she would have better luck.

"All of you will get a turn," said Mr. Peters. "We will alternate."

"Rat's knees," said Molly.

"Just keep your eye on the ball," said Jody. "And you won't have any trouble."

"That's what my dad said!" said Molly. "But it didn't help."

First Roger got up to bat. He swung the bat with every pitch. But the bat did not hit the ball. He struck out. He ran to first base, but Mr. Peters made him go back.

"Your dad is a bad pitcher," Roger muttered to Molly.

"He is not!" shouted Molly. "He played in college, he's a pro."

Roger looked like he might cry.

"Roger always has to be the best at stuff," said Mary Beth. "Or he acts awful."

Next Rachel got up to bat and hit a home run. She sailed around the bases like she did it every day. Even though her dad didn't like sports.

Some of the other Pee Wees got up to bat and missed. It did not look good. So far Rachel was the only one to score.

The other team got up to bat, and Mrs. Baker hit a home run and tied the game. The parents cheered! Then Lisa's mother hit a home run and the parents' team was ahead!

"Yea team!" shouted Tim's uncle and Mr. White.

When it was the Pee Wees' turn, Sonny got up to bat. "Yea Stone!" chanted the Pee Wees.

Sonny actually hit the ball, but as he ran to first base he tripped on his too-long pants and fell. Mrs. Kelly threw the ball to first base and Sonny was out. The Pee Wees booed, and Sonny began to cry.

"I told you that uniform would get in your way," said his mother.

Jody was up next and swung from his wheelchair. His dad stood behind him to push the wheelchair around the bases, if Jody hit the ball. The Pee Wees cheered for Jody, but he hit a foul ball and was out. Molly was surprised that her hero could let them down! Well, even her dad wasn't perfect at everything. She knew because her mom said he couldn't change a flat tire on the car if his life depended on it.

Things did not look good for Molly's team.

In the next inning, Tim got to first base. Then Lisa got a hit. Then Tracy got a hit. The three bases were loaded! And now Molly was up to bat!

"Yea Duff!" shouted the Pee Wees.

"Rat's knees," said Molly. If she missed the ball and struck out, they would lose the game. If she hit a home run, four players would score! It was up to her to save the day.

CHAPTER **8**

The Fat Bat to the Rescue

Molly took her bag and walked to home plate.

"Keep your eye on the ball!" called Jody. He held up his hand. He had his fingers crossed for luck.

"Hey, what's in the sack, Duff? Your lunch?" yelled Roger.

The Pee Wees laughed.

"I brought my own bat," said Molly. "The others are too thin."

Molly reached into her bag. She took out her fat bat. She grabbed it by the handle and swung it back and forth,

75

ready for the pitch. The team was counting on her, and now just maybe she could do it!

The Pee Wees stared at her bat.

Mr. Duff, the pitcher, stared.

The other parents stared.

"That's a tennis racket!" shouted Rachel. "You can't use a tennis racket to hit a baseball!"

"Why not?" asked Molly. "It's just like a baseball bat only fatter."

Roger hee-hawed like a donkey. "It's not legal! Hey, she's out!" he shouted. "Get her out of the game."

"She's on our team, and she can use what she wants!" said Ashley, stamping her foot. "You can't hit the ball," she reminded Roger. "You ought to be glad if Molly can."

"I never read in any rules that it was illegal to use a tennis racket to hit the ball," said Jody. "Have you, Mr. Peters?"

Mr. Peters had to admit he had not read that you could *not* use a tennis racket.

No one had. Mr. Duff finally threw the ball, and Molly hit it with her fat bat! The first time she tried! It went high and it went far! It flew over the trees and out of the park! Molly threw down her fat bat and ran around the bases.

Tim scored and Lisa scored and Tracy scored! Then Molly ran across home plate, and the Pee Wees had won the game!

"Molly, Molly, she's our man!" chanted the Pee Wees.

Jody's dad boosted Molly up on his shoulders and carried her off the field while everyone whistled and shouted and clapped.

"You won the game for us!" said Jody. "That was really good thinking."

Jody was such a good friend! He had helped her win. It didn't matter as much to her, now that she wasn't handicapped too. She didn't need a wheelchair to get attention. She was a hero without wheels! It felt good.

Even Roger acted pleased, thought Molly. But he did remind her that he still thought it was illegal.

"I think Molly ought to get a tennis badge, as well as a baseball badge!" said Jody, laughing.

Dear Jody! What a good friend!

Everyone went back to Mrs. Peters's house. She and Mr. Peters and the Stones served coffee and milk and fruit juice and snacks to everyone there. Then Mrs. Peters rapped on the table and held up the badges.

"I think every one of the Pee Wees deserves a badge. Everyone has a scrapbook and most of you hit the ball."

When there was some booing, she added, "You all did as well as you could.

And the Pee Wees definitely won the game."

Mrs. Peters called the names of each Pee Wee, and pinned the baseball badge on each of their shirts. It was red, and it had a thin bat on it. Beside the bat was a ball.

"There's yarn in that ball," said Molly when she got her badge.

The Pee Wees laughed. Except Jody.

"She's right," he said. "Baseballs are filled with yarn, and covered with real leather."

"Molly and Jody have really done a lot of work," said Mrs. Peters. "They both know a lot about baseball!"

Molly felt warm and good all over. She had hit the ball. Even if it was with a fat bat instead of a thin bat. Jody was her friend. And she had the biggest scrapbook of all the Pee Wees.

There was only one thing that still bothered her. And that was Baby Ruth. Molly had to find out how a little baby girl named after a candy bar could hit 714 home runs!

She waved her hand to ask Mrs. Peters. As she was waving it, Brett Brady came up to her. She had not even known he was there!

"Congratulations," he said to her. "You were a regular Babe Ruth out there today. You know, he was a hero too. He played with the New York Yankees for fifteen years!"

He? thought Molly. Brett called Baby Ruth *he!* How could a man be called Ruth?

"There won't be another like the old Babe," Brett went on. "But you were close. Maybe we should name a candy bar after you! The Babe-Duff bar!"

"Molly?" said Mrs. Peters. "Did you have a question?"

Molly didn't realize her hand was still up!

"No," she said. "Not anymore."

So Ruth wasn't a baby after all. And she wasn't a girl and she wasn't named after a candy bar! The candy bar was named after her!

Rat's knees! You learned something new every single day when you were a Pee Wee Scout!

Pee Wee Scout Song
(to the tune of "Old MacDonald Had a Farm")

Scouts are helpers, Scouts have fun,
Pee Wee, Pee Wee Scouts!
We sing and play when work is done,
Pee Wee, Pee Wee Scouts!

With a good deed here,
And an errand there,
Here a hand, there a hand,
Everywhere a good hand.

Scouts are helpers, Scouts have fun,
Pee Wee, Pee Wee Scouts!

☆ Pee Wee Scout Pledge ☆

We love our country
And our home,
Our school and neighbors too.

As Pee Wee Scouts
We pledge our best
In everything we do.